TURN TO THE BACK FOR A HELPFUL NAVIGATION GUIDE FOR PARENTS

More support materials available on our website flyingstartbooks.com/parents

So Fast
and Other Stories

A Red Rocket Readers Collection

Contents

1

TURN TO THE BACK FOR A HELPFUL NAVIGATION GUIDE FOR PARENTS

More support materials available on our website flyingstartbooks.com/parents

Collected edition first published in 2018 by Red Rocket Readers, an imprint of Flying Start Books Ltd.
Individual tItles first published in 2004 by Red Rocket Readers, an imprint of Flying Start Books Ltd.
13/45 Karepiro Drive, Auckland 0932, New Zealand.

So Fast. Story © Pam Holden, Illustrations © Philip Webb
Big Animals. © Pam Holden, Illustrations © Pauline Whimp
Going Up. Story © Pam Holden, Illustrations © Kelvin Hawley
Hoppity Hop. Story © Pam Holden, Illustrations © Sandra Morris
See Me Ride. Story © Pam Holden, Illustrations © Jacqueline East
Let's Play Ball. Story © Pam Holden, Illustrations © Philip Webb
Stickybeak the Parrot. Story © Pam Holden, Illustrations © Jacqueline East
What Can Fly? Story © Pam Holden, Illustrations © Sandra Cammell
ISBN 978-1-77654-196-6
Printed in India

So Fast

written by Pam Holden
illustrated by Philip Webb

Look at the motorcycle
going fast.

Look at the horse
going fast.

Look at the fire engine going fast.

9

Look at the race car
going fast.

Look at the rocket
going fast.

13

Look at the police ca
going fast.

Look at the shark
going fast.

Look at the boat
going **very** fast!

Big Animals

written by Pam Holden
illustrated by Pauline Whimp

"I am big,"
said the kangaroo.

20

"I am big,"
said the horse.

"I am big," said the bear.

24

"I am big,"
said the gorilla.

"I am big,"
said the crocodile.

"I am big,"
said the whale.

31

"I am big," said the elephant.

"I am very big,"
said the dinosaur.

Going Up

written by Pam Holden
illustrated by Kelvin Hawley

I go up the tree.

I go up the mountair

I go up the rope.

I go up the hill.

I go up the steps.

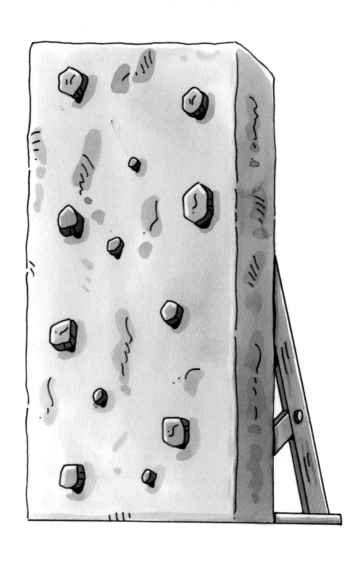

I go up the wall.

47

I go up the ladder.

I go down the slide.
Wheee!

Hoppity Hop

written by Pam Holden
illustrated by Sandra Morris

"We can hop,"
said the frogs.

"We can hop,"
said the rabbits.

"We can hop,"
said the penguins.

"We can hop," said
the grasshoppers.

"We can hop,"
said the birds.

"We can hop,"
said the kangaroos.

"We can hop,"
said the children.

1 2 3 4 5
6 7 8 Hop!

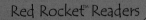

See Me Ride

written by Pam Holden
illustrated by Jacqueline East

I like to ride
on this bike.

I like to ride
on this train.

I like to ride
on this boat.

I like to ride
on this elephant.

I like to ride
on this horse.

I like to ride
on this plane.

I like to ride
on this rocket.

I like to ride
on this shoulder.

Let's Play Ball

written by Pam Holden
illustrated by Philip Webb

We like to throw
balls.

We like to hit
balls.

We like to kick
balls.

We like to bounce
balls.

We like to bowl
balls.

We like to catch
balls.

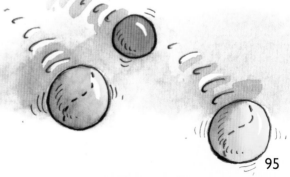

We like to roll balls.

We like to juggle
balls. Ooooops!

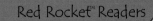

Stickybeak the Parrot

written by Pam Holden
illustrated by Jacqueline East

He likes to fly
a lot.

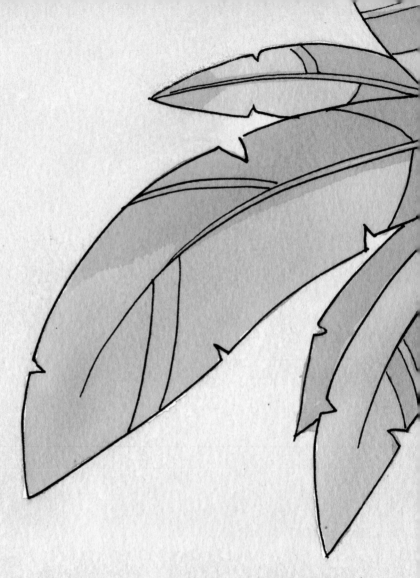

He likes to climb
a lot.

He likes to eat
a lot.

He likes to drink
a lot.

He likes to sing
a lot.

He likes to swing
a lot.

He likes to scratch a lot.

He likes to talk
a lot. Hello, hello.

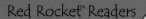

What Can Fly?

written by Pam Holden
illustrated by Sandra Cammell

A bird can fly.

A plane can fly.

A fly can fly.

A bat can fly.

A butterfly can fly.

A duck can fly.

A bee can fly.

And a bee can sting!

NAVIGATION GUIDE FOR PARENTS

Support and enhance the work your child is doing at school with additional practice at every level.

Follow these steps to get them off to a flying start with literacy and learning:

1. **Picture walk and talk before you read** to introduce each story, its title and what it is about. Take a page-by-page picture walk to introduce new concepts and talk about what might happen in the story.

2. **Read together every day.** Red Rocket Readers Collections are ideal for a week of home reading practice, reading one story each day.

3. **Choose the right books!** A funny story, an interesting topic, and the right reading level – children need books that they can manage successfully and enjoy.

4. **Be positive!** It's essential that early learning-to-read experiences are positive, so praise all efforts.

These vital steps will set children up for early success!

Read more at flyingstartbooks.com/parents

INTRODUCING THE STORIES IN THIS COLLECTION

So Fast

"This story is called **So Fast.** It's about lots of different things that can go fast. Do you like going fast? What can go very fast? Look at these things going fast."

Sight words: **at   going   Look   the**

Big Animals

"This story is called **Big Animals.** It's about different kinds of big animals. Do you know some very big animals? Are they bigger than you? Which animal is the biggest?"

Sight words: **am   big   I   said   the**

Going Up

"This story is called **Going Up.** It's about boys and girls climbing up things. Do you like climbing? Can you climb up high? Where do you go to climb? How high can you go?"

Sight words: **down   go   I   the   up**

Hoppity Hop

"This story is called **Hoppity Hop.** It's about animals that can hop. Can you hop? How do you hop? Can you hop on your left foot? Can you hop on your right foot? Lots of animals can hop too. Do you know which animals can hop?"

Sight words: **can** **said** **the** **We**

See Me Ride

"This story is called **See Me Ride.** It's about a parrot called Stickybeak who likes to go for rides on different things. What do you like to ride on? Which one of these rides would you like best?"

Sight words: **I** **like** **me** **on** **see** **this** **to**

Let's Play Ball

"This story is called **Let's Play Ball.** It's about games that we can play with a ball. Can you catch a ball? What else can you do with a ball? There are lots of different kinds of balls. What games can we play with balls? What do you like to do with a ball?"

Sight words: **it** **like** **to** **We**

Stickybeak the Parrot

"This story is called **Stickybeak the Parrot.** It's about Stickybeak the parrot and what he likes to do. Have you seen a parrot? What do parrots like to do? He is busy doing all the things that parrots like to do."

Sight words: **a** **He** **likes** **to**

What Can Fly?

"This story is called **What Can Fly?** It's about animals and other things that can fly. Have you been flying in a plane? Was it fun to go flying? Do you know lots of things that can fly?"

Sight words: **a** **A** **and** **can**

Look For Other Titles Available Now:

A BOOK FOR EVERY READER!

Learning to read is a complex process, that draws upon an extensive knowledge base and repertoire of strategies. Each essential step must be secure before progressing to the next level.

Award winning Red Rocket Readers feature controlled-language that is reading level appropriate. With a 50/50 split of fiction and non-fiction texts, supported by attractive illustrations for fiction and stunning photography supporting the non-fiction texts, there's a book for every reader.

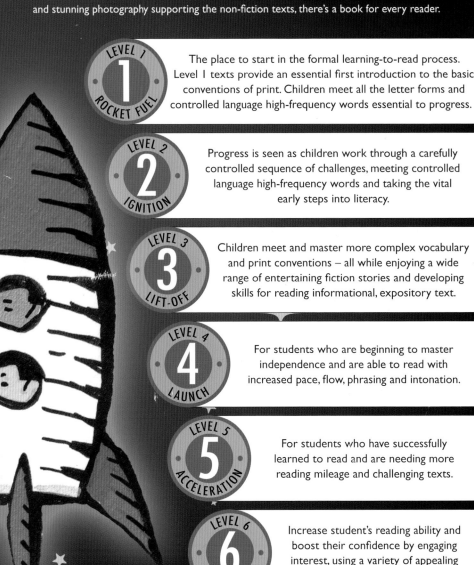

LEVEL 1
1
ROCKET FUEL

The place to start in the formal learning-to-read process. Level 1 texts provide an essential first introduction to the basic conventions of print. Children meet all the letter forms and controlled language high-frequency words essential to progress.

LEVEL 2
2
IGNITION

Progress is seen as children work through a carefully controlled sequence of challenges, meeting controlled language high-frequency words and taking the vital early steps into literacy.

LEVEL 3
3
LIFT-OFF

Children meet and master more complex vocabulary and print conventions — all while enjoying a wide range of entertaining fiction stories and developing skills for reading informational, expository text.

LEVEL 4
4
LAUNCH

For students who are beginning to master independence and are able to read with increased pace, flow, phrasing and intonation.

LEVEL 5
5
ACCELERATION

For students who have successfully learned to read and are needing more reading mileage and challenging texts.

LEVEL 6
6
BOOST

Increase student's reading ability and boost their confidence by engaging interest, using a variety of appealing text types and genres.